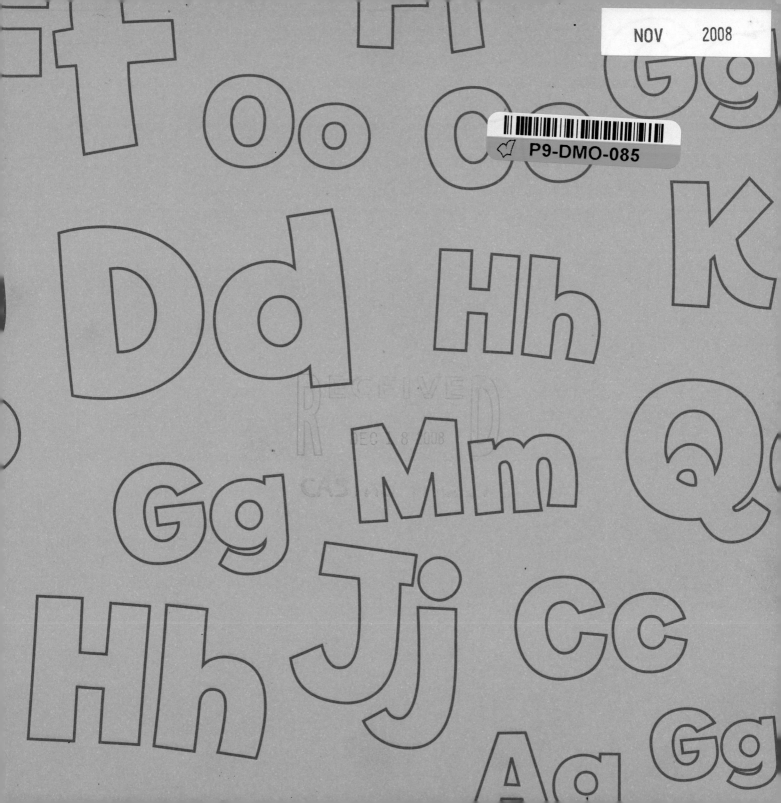

C is for California

written by kids for kids

A is for **Alcatraz**

On an island in the San Francisco Bay,
Alcatraz is a place where prisoners used to stay.

B

is for **Beach**

I run on the beach with the spray on my face.
I dive in the sea with breathtaking grace.

C

is for

Cinco de Mayo

The fifth of May is a
Mexican celebration,
that spreads across
the whole wide nation!

D
is for

Disneyland

A place where
families have fun,
Mickey Mouse, rides, and
parades in the sun.

E is for Earthquake

When you hear a RUMBLE

buildings may begin to crumble!

F is for

Fisherman's Wharf

Fishermen's boats by the dock.
Seagulls flying in a flock.

G is for Gold Rush

The gold rush was in California in 1848.
James Marshall found the shiny bait.

H

is for **Hearst Castle**

This castle has many fountains and pools,
and the water sparkles like beautiful jewels.

I is for

Indigenous People

Native Americans
painted the rock's face.
Now it marks a
sacred place.

J is for

Father Junipero Serra

In San Diego
he got permission
to build California's
first mission.

K is for King's Canyon

Mountains with snow where flowers grow,
misty air above and the valley below.

L

is for **Los Angeles**

Los Angeles the city of lights
is like a blanket of stars at night.

M is for Monterey Bay Aquarium

In the aquarium jelly fish drift,
sharks and eels, the ocean's gift.

N is for **Napa Valley**

Grapes growing on the vines
make California's wines.

O

is for Orange

Oranges ripening
in a big field
soon are going to be
picked and peeled.

P is for **Poppy**

The Golden State flower
glowing in the sunset hour.

Q is for

Quail

The California quail
has a plume
that looks like
a flower in bloom.

R is for

Redwood

The tall redwood tree
stands firm and proud
hanging over us like
a luminescent cloud.

S is for

Sacramento

Our state capital
is Sacramento,
where people make laws
and ideas flow.

T is for **Tahoe**

Tahoe has a sparkling lake
that is like icing on a cake.

U
is for
Ursus Californicus
High on the flag is a grizzly bear.
The whistling wind is ruffling its hair.

CALIFORNIA REPUBLIC

V

is for **Central Valley**

All types of crops are harvested each year.
Much of America's food is grown here.

W

is for **Wind**

Wind makes energy,
wind makes power.
It gains more force
with every hour.

X is for e**X**tremes

No matter if the mountains or
the desert fill your dreams
pick snow or sun, both kinds of fun
are found in our extremes.

y is for **Yosemite**

An ancient glacier carved Half Dome's face.
Now the snow covers the mountains like lace.

Z is for San Diego Zoo

I see a polar bear through the glass.

He stares at me as I pass.

Who Knew?

Alcatraz

This tiny island located in the middle of San Francisco Bay is also known as "The Rock." In its 29 years of operation as a federal prison, not a single prisoner successfully escaped, although some inmates certainly gave it a shot! Thirty-six prisoners tried to escape and one man tried twice. Their most famous prisoner was the notorious Al Capone.

Beach

The 1,100-mile-long California coastline is home to 118 beach cities and 450 beaches. Fifteen million people live near the state's beaches and enjoy the surfing, sailing, swimming, and magnificent scenery that these beaches offer.

Cinco de Mayo

While you might know that Cinco de Mayo commemorates the victory of Mexican forces over French forces in the Battle of Puebla in 1862, it took another 50 years for the Mexicans to gain their independence. Cinco de Mayo is more of a celebration of Mexican culture and unity than anything else. And do they know how to party! Dancing, mariachi bands, great food: it's a fiesta you don't want to miss!

Disneyland

This world-famous theme park opened in 1955, making it 16 years older than its sister, Disneyworld, in Florida. Some 515 million people have visited Disneyland. That's more than 10 times the population of the whole state of California! Walt Disney had his own office on the second floor of a building on Main Street, USA, and you can see a light still burning there in honor of the creator of Mickey Mouse and his friends.

Earthquake

The 800-mile San Andreas Fault is one of the many fault lines that runs through the state and because of it, California has small earthquakes almost constantly! One of the biggest, not just in California but in the entire country, happened in 1906. This earthquake and the fire caused by it destroyed most of San Francisco and is considered one of the worst natural disasters in American history.

Fisherman's Wharf

San Francisco's most popular tourist attraction is known for its historic waterfront, fun shops, and barking sea lions. That's right, sea lions. Hundreds of them took over a boat marina and have never left. They lie there barking and basking in the sun. It is quite a sight to see.

Gold Rush

The California Gold Rush began on January 24, 1848, when gold was discovered at Sutter's Mill in Coloma. As a result more than 300,000 people came to California from all over the world in search of their fortunes. They were called the 49ers and about one hundred years later, San Francisco chose this name for the city's first professional sports team.

Hearst Castle

Hearst Castle was the vacation home of newspaper owner William Randolph Hearst and covers 250,000 acres. That is 17 times the size of Manhattan Island! All for one family! At first it was used as a camping ground for the family, but as it grew Hearst got tired of camping and built guest houses in addition to the castle, which includes 56 bedrooms, 41 fireplaces, and 61 bathrooms.

Facts about the

Indigenous People

California has the largest number of Native Americans of any state in the United States. Some of those tribes include the Pomo, Modoc, and Ohlone.

Father Junipero Serra

Father Junipero Serra was born in Mallorca, Spain, in 1713. He left for the New World in 1750 and founded the first of California's 21 missions in 1769. The missions were built so that they were a day's ride by horseback from each other.

King's Canyon

King's Canyon National Park was established in 1940 and is home to the largest natural giant sequoia grove in the world. The highest point in the park, North Palisade, is so high that it is only snow-free from June to October.

Los Angeles

Los Angeles is the largest city in California and the second largest in the United States. It has a population of almost four million people. Its nickname is the "City of Angels."

Monterey Bay Aquarium

The MBA is located in a former sardine cannery on Cannery Row in Monterey. They have won tons of awards for their incredible exhibits, including California giant kelp, black-footed penguins, and all sorts of cool interactive displays for young marine biologists.

Napa Valley

This beautiful valley is world famous for its wines. Almost 4.7 million people visit Napa Valley each year, making it one of the most popular tourist destinations in California, second only to Disneyland.

Orange

Spanish explorers brought oranges, which originated in China, to California in the 18th century. The California navel orange is one of the most popular kinds of oranges in the United States but did you know that it was created by mistake? A normal sweet orange tree mutated to create the seedless orange that gets its name from the part on the bottom of the fruit that looks like your belly button!

Poppy

The California poppy covers the hillsides of the state from February through October. Native Americans used the poppy petals for making medicine and its seeds were used in cooking. Californians love their state flower so much they celebrate California Poppy Day every April 6.

Quail

The state bird of California is the very sociable quail. It gathers daily in small flocks known as coveys to take dust baths and forage for its food, which consists of seeds, grass, small berries, and insects.

great state of California

Redwood

The sequoia or redwood is the tallest tree in the world and can live up to 2,200 years. Redwood forests provide habitat for a variety of mammals, birds, reptiles, and amphibians.

Sacramento

When gold was discovered in 1848, the rush of people to Sacramento and its surrounding areas was recorded as the largest human migration in history. Some of the buildings built in the 1860s are still standing and you can see them in Old Town Sacramento.

Tahoe

This freshwater lake lies right on the border of California and Nevada and is the second-deepest lake in the United States. It is known for its clear blue-green water and for the beautiful Sierra Nevada Mountain Range surrounding it.

Ursus Californicus

The California grizzly bear was named the state animal in 1953, more than 30 years after the last grizzly was seen in the state. The grizzly can weigh up to 800 pounds and measure up to eight feet tall when standing.

Central Valley

The Central Valley is one of the most productive agricultural areas in the world. The valley stretches 400 miles from north to south and is bordered on the east by the Sierra Nevada Mountains and on the west by the Coast Range. It is known as the "fruit basket of the world."

Wind

Since ancient times, people have used the wind's energy to make life easier. Today California uses more wind to generate electricity than any other state. Scientists are studying ways to build windmills in the Pacific Ocean in order to produce energy.

eXtremes

Many days during the summer both the coldest and hottest recorded temperatures in the country are reached less than 100 miles apart in California. California is home to both the highest (Mount Whitney) and the lowest (Death Valley) points in the United States. Now those are extremes!

yosemite

President Abraham Lincoln signed a bill in 1864 making Yosemite the first piece of scenic land set aside just to protect and preserve it for the enjoyment of Americans. Yosemite didn't become a national park until 1890 but it was well guarded by the state of California until that time.

San Diego Zoo

The San Diego Zoo is one of the largest in the world with a population of 4,000-plus animals and more than 800 species. The zoo's pride and joy is their giant pandas. The first giant panda born in North America to survive to adulthood, Hua Mei, was born at the San Diego Zoo.

Photo by Gail Newman

Photo by Gail Newman

The poems in this book were written in California Poets in the Schools (cpits.org) workshops conducted by Gail Newman.

Thanks to the staff and parents of Alvarado Elementary School and Claire Lilienthal School, K-8 for their support of the poetry program.

A Zalika Cheruvattam
B Alejandra Arroyo
C Norbu Globus
D Tiana O'Neal
E Miranda Finestone
F Lucia Tisker
G Isaac Noh
H Samantha Gong
I Paul Levinson

J Cian Modena-Hayden
K Maxwell Nesbet
L Ian Lipanovich
M Sam Lax
N Altea Biarchi-Bellfort
O Taro Yamamoto
P Caio Driver
Q Rosie Lee
R Eli Kapsack

S Christopher Begler &
   Zachary Louie
T Jordan De Angelo
U Antonia Duble
V Liam Thirtyacre
W Andrew Pearce
X Teresa Attridge (not pictured)
Y Naser Suleiman
Z Natalia Alegre

Library of Congress Cataloging-in-Publication Data
C is for California.
    p. cm.
 ISBN 978-0-88240-749-4 (hardbound)
 1. California—Juvenile literature. 2. Alphabet books—Juvenile literature.
 F861.3.C23 2008
 979.4—dc22

                        2008009593

WestWinds Press® An imprint of Graphic Arts Center Publishing Company
P.O. Box 10306, Portland, Oregon 97296-0306
503/226-2402 • www.gacpc.com

President: Charles M. Hopkins
Associate Publisher: Douglas A. Pfeiffer
Editorial Staff: Timothy W. Frew, Jean Andrews, Kathy Howard, Jean Bond-Slaughter
Production Coordinator: Susan Dupèrè
Editor: Gail Newman
Designer: Vicki Knapton

Printed in China